by Sarah Hines Stephens

POOCHES OF POWER

illustrated by
Art Baltazar

Batman created by Bob Kane

Superman created by
Jerry Siegel and Joe Shuster

Raintree

Starring...

ACE
THE BAT-HOUND

KRYPTO
THE SUPER-DOG

THE BAD NEWS BIRDS

BATMAN

WADDLES

ARTIE PUFFIN

GRIFF

THE PENGUIN

CONTENTS

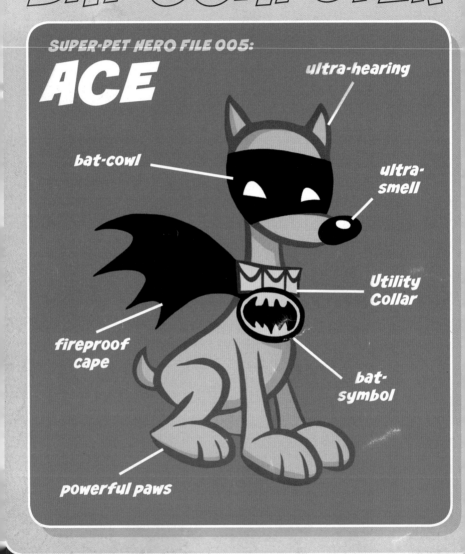

BATCAVE
BAT-COMPUTER

SUPER-PET HERO FILE 005:

ACE

ultra-hearing

bat-cowl

ultra-smell

Utility Collar

fireproof cape

bat-symbol

powerful paws

BATMAN

Species: Bat-Hound

Place of birth: Gotham City

Age: unknown

Favourite food:
Crime Fighter Crunchies

Bio: Batman found Ace while solving a case. Unable to find the owner, the Dark Knight kept the dog and nicknamed him "The Bat-Hound". Ace considers himself Batman's partner, *not* his pet.

Chapter 1

WHIFF OF TROUBLE

Ace the Bat-Hound stretched his legs. He settled down at billionaire Bruce Wayne's feet. The two crime fighters were back from their nightly rounds and enjoying their morning. While their butler, Alfred, served tea, Bruce and Ace relaxed with the paper.

This morning, the news was not helping Ace relax. There was something fishy about the headline. **"Missing Fish at Sardine Factory"**, Bruce read aloud.  Those words made the fur on Ace's neck stand up.

MISSING FISH AT SARDINE FACTORY

Ace knew the factory well. It was located on the Gotham City docks – a favourite hangout for thieves.

Batman and Ace often patrolled the area. Whenever they passed the factory, the workers would toss Ace a sardine treat.

Lately, however, the workers did not have a fish to spare. According to the paper, they did not even have enough to fill their tins. The fishermen were catching as much as always, but the factory was coming up short.

Somebody must be stealing the fish between the fishing boats and the factory, Ace thought. *But who? And how?* The questions bothered Ace like an itchy flea under his Utility Collar.

The moment Bruce left for work, Ace streaked through  his dog door. He headed over to the Gotham City docks.

When he arrived, everything looked and smelled normal. Still, something did not feel right.

Most of the fishing boats were out at sea. The crowd of shady people that hung around at night had turned in. The factory workers had not yet arrived for the morning shift. It was so quiet. *Too quiet,* the Bat-Hound thought.

As he moved closer to the factory, Ace slowed down. With his canine hearing, he sensed someone coming.

BEEP! BEEP! BEEP!

Suddenly, a gadget on Ace's Utility Collar sounded an alarm. It had picked up someone, or something, in the shadows by the back doors of the factory.

FWOOSH!

"**Krypto!**" Ace greeted his friend the Super-Dog. "I thought I might find you here."

With his super-sniffing powers, **Krypto** had smelled trouble on the docks long before anyone else. He had already been nosing around for clues and found something.

SNIFF! SNIFF!

"I sniffed out some evidence," the Super-Dog barked. **"Follow me!"**

Krypto soared up to the rooftop of a warehouse connected to the factory.

WOOOOSH!

"Up here," he said. "Need a lift?"

Ace did not bother to answer. The Bat-Hound could not fly. He had his own way of getting around. Taking huge leaps, he made his way up. He jumped from a pile of crates, to a cargo bin, and on to the roof.

Once there, Ace only needed a second to understand the clue Krypto had found. The feathers lying on the rooftop could mean only one thing . . .

"The Bad News Birds," Ace growled.

Chapter 2

FOWL PLAY

The feathers Krypto had found were a sure sign of **Batman's evil enemy the Penguin!** His sidekicks must have been spending time on the docks.

The blue feather belonged to **Waddles,** the evil penguin. The white-tipped vulture feather was **Griff's.**

The black feathers had to be **Artie the puffin's.** Together, the three birds were a flock of trouble.

"Does this mean Penguin is behind the missing fish?" Krypto asked.

Ace's eyes narrowed. The criminal was behind a lot of Gotham's crime. Ace wanted to pin the blame for the missing fish on him, too. But he did not have enough proof. Besides, Ace did not think Penguin could make enough money stealing sardines to feed his greedy appetite.

The Bat-Hound needed more
information before he could point
a paw at Penguin. Luckily, he and
Krypto had a bird's-eye view of the
docks. As they checked the area, the
Dog Duo heard squawks from inside.

Ace and Krypto looked through a
skylight into the warehouse below.
Through the glass, they saw a black
and white creature. It wore a top hat
and was enjoying a slice of pizza. **It
was the Penguin!**

"There he is!" Krypto growled.

"Let's get him." The Super-Dog was ready to break the glass. He wanted to catch the villain while he ate.

"Hold on," said the Bat-Hound. **"We need proof first."**

"Isn't that proof enough?" Krypto asked, pointing below. Penguin's pizza was piled high with sardines – the same fish missing from the factory.

"One giant pizza doesn't explain thousands of missing fish," said Ace.

Ace's eyes locked on a wobbling bird delivering Penguin's lunch. **Waddles!** "But maybe *he* can help," growled the Bat-Hound.

Ace watched Waddles walk over to his boss with another sardine pizza. Penguin gave it a sniff. Then he sent the pizza sailing across the room.

"I'm sick of pizza," Penguin said. He waved his deadly umbrella. "And I'm sick of hiding. When are we going to be ready?"

Ace put his head closer to the glass.

He knew who Penguin was hiding

from. He was hiding from Batman.

The super hero had gathered enough

evidence from other crimes to lock

Penguin up for good.

"Take it easy, boss," Waddles said.

He scooped the fish off the floor. "It's

not so bad here."

"Not so bad?" Penguin screeched.

"Beats prison," Waddles replied.

The Penguin tapped his umbrella on

the floor angrily. Waddles had a point.

Rotting in jail would be worse.

"We need to lay low for a little

longer," Waddles said, backing out of

the room. **"We're almost ready to go."**

"Ready to go where?" Ace asked himself.

BEEP!

The Bat-Hound pushed a button on his collar. He sent an electronic message to the **Batcave.** He had recorded everything he had just seen. The video would alert Batman to the Penguin's location.

"Can we get him now?" Krypto asked.

"Soon," Ace said in a low growl. "Two slices of pizza are only part of the pie. We still need more proof."

The Bat-Hound hoped to get to the bottom of this factory caper. As he spoke, Ace watched Waddles walk over to the door.

"Follow that bird!" he directed the Super-Dog. "Waddles might lead us to the next clue."

FWOOOSH!

Krypto flew from the rooftop after the evil bird.

While the Super-Dog kept an eye
on Waddles, Ace investigated. On
the top of the factory, the Bat-Hound
spotted a fish-sorting machine. An
attached funnel was where fishermen
unloaded their catch of the day.

Ace looked inside. Though the day was warming up, a cool breeze blew out of the machine and across Ace's nose. Just like that, he knew exactly where the rest of the Bad News Birds were cooling their heels.

Ace leapt down from the roof the way he had come up. He needed a way inside the factory. The second story window would work just fine.

Ace pushed a button on his collar. He launched a **Batarang** and wire.

CLANK! The Batarang caught on the edge of the roof. Ace pulled himself up the wire and inside.

The factory was dark. Ace slipped through the shadows. He stopped in front of a locked freezer door.

"Waddles is inside the freezer," Krypto said, walking up beside Ace.

"And the other birds?" Ace asked.

Krypto took a look with his **X-ray vision.** "Griff and Artie are in there, too," he said.

The three birds were resting beside what looked like a long slide. They had been using the funnel to steal the sardines!

"We've got to get in there," Ace growled. **"Now!"**

Chapter 3

IN THE CAN

Krypto focused his **heat vision** on the steel door. Laser beams blasted out of his eyes. They melted the door's hinges. *TSSSssss!*

The door hit the ground. CLANG! The birds looked up to see Ace and Krypto blocking any chance of escape.

"**Help!**" shouted Waddles, rolling on to his feet.

Artie blinked, gripping fish in his beak. Griff shivered in silence.

ARF! ARF!

"The gig is up, sardine snatchers," Ace growled. "We've only got one choice to make. Should we hand you over to the police now? Or should we let your boss punish you first?"

"**Punish us for what?**" Artie asked.

"**Foiling his escape plan,**" Ace said.

BLEEP! Suddenly, a whistle blew outside the factory. Artie smiled. Before the Dog Duo knew what was happening, ten tonnes of fish came sliding down the funnel.

SPLOOSH!

The fishy flood picked up the birds and dogs. It carried them out of the freezer door and on to the factory floor.

Artie was the first one back on his feet. The puffin took out his pair of **ice dice**. He gave them a roll.

Ace showed his teeth. No matter what numbers Artie rolled, the results would be ugly. When the dice stopped, two dots stared up from the cubes. The high-tech weapon froze Krypto and Ace in their tracks.

"So long, you mangy mutts!" Artie called out.

Griff pulled Waddles to his feet. They sprinted out of the factory. Artie grabbed his dice and flapped after them. They were getting away!

"We have to stop them!" Ace barked. He could barely move his frozen snout.

Once again, Krypto came to the rescue. Using his heat vision, he quickly thawed himself and Ace.

"You go that way," Ace said.

Krypto took off like a shot. Ace paused for a moment. The Bat-Hound had spotted an escape hatch.

Lifting the door to the hatch with his teeth, Ace dropped into a tube. He slid into the fishy darkness.

After a moment, Ace splashed to a stop in a large room filled with tanks. He had fallen so far down, he thought he must be underground.

Then suddenly, the Bat-Hound knew that he was underwater. **He was inside Penguin's secret submarine!**

All around him, the Dog Detective saw large barrels of fish oil. The barrels were connected by tubes to the sub's high-tech fuel tanks. By turning sardines into oil, Penguin planned to power his sub and escape Gotham.

"Not if I can help it," Ace growled.

The Bat-Hound quickly left the

sub through a small hatch. Using his

special air hose, Ace swam underwater.

He headed back to the docks to stop

Penguin's plan.

Still wet with ocean water, Ace entered the factory. He spotted the bad birds hiding in the rafters. **"Thought you'd fly the coop, did you?"** he barked.

Ace pulled a tiny grenade from his collar. He removed the pin and kicked the explosive away with his back legs.

The noise startled everyone in the factory. No one was hurt, but it gave Ace the chance he needed.

The Bat-Hound set his torch on a table. He turned it on. Then he launched a Batarang at the light switch. **FWIP!** The room went dark, except for the single spotlight.

Using his paws, Ace created a shadow in the shape of Penguin on the wall. Then he pushed a button on his Utility Collar. He played back the voice recording he had made earlier.

"You're done for!" the Penguin's voice boomed through the room.

"Ah!" screamed Waddles, Artie, and Griff. The Bad News Birds ran in all directions. They tripped over each other with fright. **SQUAWK!**

Ace's plan worked perfectly. Without waiting, he tossed his Batarang. He tied the birds together. Then he swung them on to a nearby machine.

"Nice work," said a deep voice behind Ace. It was **Batman.** He stepped into the factory, holding on to the Penguin. "Looks like we're both out bird hunting today."

The Penguin growled. He struggled to get away. The villain did not stand a chance. **"How'd you find me anyway, Batty?"** Penguin asked.

"Let's just say a little bird told me," Batman replied.

Penguin spotted his wingmen tied up on the cleaning and tinning machine. He struggled harder. "I would have been long gone if you lousy fish-eaters hadn't been eating all of my fuel!" Penguin shouted.

Griff, Waddles, and Artie were swept into the sardine machine. The criminal turned his glare on Ace. **"Is this mutt yours?"** he asked Batman.

"No," Batman replied. **"We just run in the same pack."**

Ace held his head high. But this was no time to celebrate. The job was not wrapped up yet. He was beginning to worry about Krypto. He had not seen his friend since they had escaped from the freezer. The Super-Dog never missed out on the action.

"We'll never fit," Artie moaned as the birds came out from the cleaner, their feathers plucked. The next stop on the belt was where fish were pressed into tiny tins.

"Not to worry," said a voice outside.

Krypto was back, and he had a surprise! The Super-Dog flew in fast. He was carrying a sardine tin large enough to fit the flock. He scooped up the birds and stuck them inside.

"Don't you know, stealing is foul play?" Krypto asked, wagging his tail.

"That's right," Ace agreed. "We're putting you dirty birds right where you belong."

"In the can!" they both barked.

THE END

KNOW YOUR

 Krypto

Streaky

Beppo

 Comet

 Ace

 Jumpa

 Whatzit

 B'dg

 Storm

 Topo

 Ark

 Hoppy

 Paw Pooch

 Bull Dog

 Chameleon Collie

 Hot Dog

These are **HERO PETS.**

 Tail Terrier

 Tusky Husky

GLOSSARY

Batarang high-tech weapon used by the Bat-Hound

evidence information or facts that help prove something or make you believe that something is true

patrol walk around an area to protect it or keep an eye on people

sardine small saltwater fish, often sold in a tin as food

sidekick partner, or a person who works for and helps out another person

Utility Collar thin band worn around the Bat-Hound's neck, which contains all his secret gadgets

MEET THE AUTHOR

Sarah Hines Stephens

Sarah Hines Stephens has written more than 60 books for children about all kinds of characters, from Jedi to princesses. When she is not writing, gardening, or saving the world by teaching people about recycling, Sarah enjoys spending time with her heroic husband, two kids, and super friends.

MEET THE ILLUSTRATOR

Eisner Award-winner Art Baltazar

Art Baltazar defines cartoons and comics not only as a style of art, but as a way of life. Art is the creative force behind *The New York Times* best-selling, Eisner Award-winning, DC Comics series Tiny Titans and the co-writer for *Billy Batson and the Magic of SHAZAM!* Art draws comics and never has to leave the house. He lives with his lovely wife, Rose, big boy Sonny, little boy Gordon, and little girl Audrey.

Published by Capstone Global Library Limited, a company incorporated in England and Wales having its registered office at 7 Pilgrim Street, London, EC4V 6LB - Registered company number: 6695582

First published by Raintree in 2011
First published in India in 2012

ISBN 978 1 406 25291 0 (paperback)
16 15 14 13 12
10 9 8 7 6 5 4 3 2 1

British Library Cataloguing in Publication Data
A full catalogue record for this book is available from the British Library

Printed at Multivista Global Limited

Art Director and Designer: Bob Lentz
Editors: Donald Lemke and Vaarunika Dharmapala
Production Specialist: Michelle Biedscheid
Creative Director: Heather Kindseth
Editorial Director: Michael Dahl

www.raintreepublishers.co.uk
Email: myorders@raintreepublishers.co.uk

Bloomington, Chicago, Mankato, Oxford